EDWINA
the
EMU

☺☺☺☺☺☺☺☺☺☺☺☺☺☺☺☺☺☺☺☺☺☺☺☺

To

Holly McLachlan

From Keiraville Community Preschool

We hope when you read this book you will
remember all your friends at preschool.
We will always remember you and the fun we
had together.   2007

For ZOE and MARGOT — S.K.

Angus&Robertson
An imprint of HarperCollins*Publishers*, Australia

First published in Australia in 1996
Book Club edition 1996
This Bluegum paperback edition published in 1997
by HarperCollins*Publishers* Pty Limited
ABN 36 009 913 517
A member of the HarperCollins*Publishers* (Australia) Pty Limited Group
www.harpercollins.com.au

Text copyright © Sheena Knowles 1996
Illustrations copyright © Rod Clement 1996

The right of Sheena Knowles and Rod Clement to be identified as the
moral rights author and illustrator of this work has been asserted by them in
accordance with the *Copyright Amendment (Moral Rights) Act 2000* (Cth).

HarperCollins*Publishers*
25 Ryde Road, Pymble, Sydney NSW 2073, Australia
31 View Road, Glenfield, Auckland 10, New Zealand
77–85 Fulham Palace Road, London W6 8JB, United Kingdom
2 Bloor Street East, 20th floor, Toronto, Ontario, M4W 1A8, Canada
10 East 53rd Street, New York NY 10022, USA

National Library of Australia Cataloguing-in-Publication data:

Knowles, Sheena.
Edwina the emu.
ISBN 0 207 18914 5 (p/b).
ISBN 0 207 18913 7 (h/b).
1. Emus—Juvenile fiction. I. Clement, Rod. II. Title.
A823.3

Printed in China by Everbest Printing on 128gsm Matt Art

22 21 20 19   07 08 09 10

EDWINA
the
EMU

Sheena Knowles ✦ *Rod Clement*

Angus&Robertson

An imprint of HarperCollins*Publishers*

There once were two emus who lived in the zoo,
One was Edwina and Edward was two.
They played every day, there was never a fight
And they cuddled up close to keep warm every night.

As they sat there one day, entwining their legs,
Edwina announced, she'd laid ten little eggs.

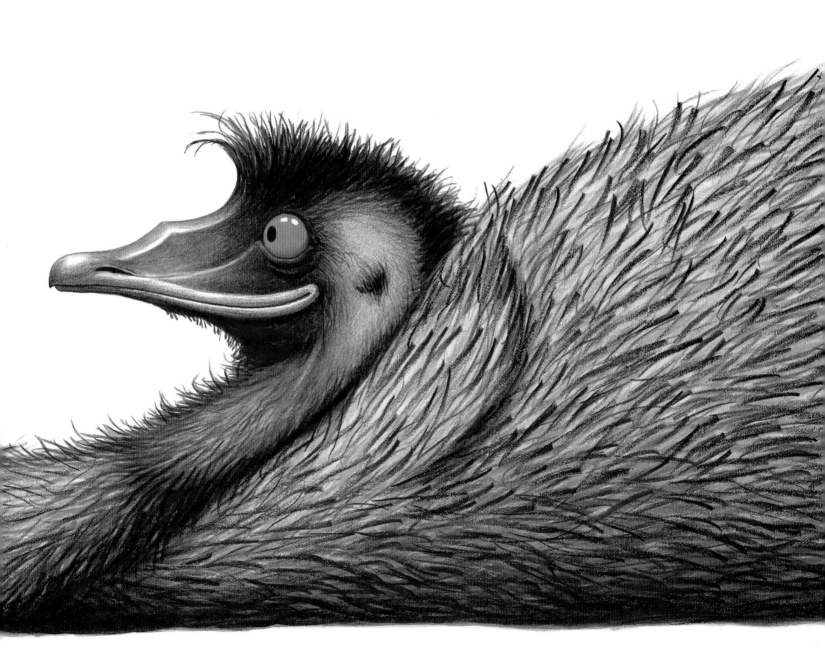

'YEEK!' shouted Edward, he seemed to be choking,
'*Ten* little emus? You've got to be joking!'
'I'm not,' said Edwina, 'but don't get depressed,
I'll look for a job, you stay on the nest.'

An ad in the paper said "Dance the Ballet—
If you've got the legs, we're willing to pay."
'Great,' said Edwina, 'that would be fine.
I'll hop on a bus and I'll be there at nine.'

The director called out for the next ballerina
And onto the stage stepped the lovely Edwina.
She whirled and she waltzed, she twirled and she leapt,
Then she twisted her legs in a grand pirouette.

'YEEK!' the man shouted, he seemed to be choking,
'An emu dance ballet? You've got to be joking!'
'I'm not,' said Edwina, 'but don't laugh at me,
I'll find the right job soon, you just wait and see.'

An ad in the paper said "Chimney to sweep—
Stick your neck out, you could make a heap."
'I will,' said Edwina, 'now this will be fun,
I'll hop on a bus and I'll be there by one.'

Up on the roof, the wind whistled about,
'I'm ready!' the lady below shouted out.
'I'll just be a minute!' Edwina called back,
Then she pushed till she popped through,
    bristled and black.

'YEEK!' said the lady, she seemed to be choking,
'An emu sweep chimneys? You've got to be joking!'
'I'm not,' said Edwina, 'but don't laugh at me,
I'll find the right job soon, you just wait and see.'

An ad in the paper said "Waiter required–
If you're quick on your feet, you're sure to be hired."

'Yes,' said Edwina, 'that's perfect for me,
I'll hop on a bus and I'll be there by three.'

Edwina served tea to a man in a hat,
'Would you like me to bring you a meal with that?'
'Yes,' said the man, 'I'll have sausages, fried,
With a couple of nice runny eggs on the side.'

'YEEK!' said Edwina, she seemed to be choking,
'You want to eat EGGS? You've got to be joking!'
'I'm not,' said the man, 'eating eggs is the best,
Once I ate ten of them, straight from a nest.'

Edwina ran out, she ran into the street,
It was true when she said she was quick on her feet.
'Taxi!' she cried, 'take me home, make it fast,
I know what the right job for me is – at last!'

It was late when Edwina got back to the nest,
'You're late,' muttered Edward, 'and I need a rest.'
'You're right,' said Edwina, 'from now on we share.
I'll sit on the nest, you pull up a chair.'

There once were twelve emus who lived in the zoo,
One was Edwina and Edward was two.
Then Fluffy and Scruffy and Sniffly-Sneeze,

And Fatty and Footloose and Knobbly Knees,
And Lollypop-Legs and Shortening and Squeak,
And the last little emu?

They called that one …

Yeek!